Tom

Huck

CLASSIC ILLUSTRATED™

B BERKLEY/ FIRST PUBLISHING **1F**

Mark Twain

The Adventures of
TOM SAWYER

adapted and illustrated by
Michael Ploog

lettered by
Willie Schubert

"**M**ost of the adventures recorded in this book really occurred," Mark Twain wrote in his preface to **The Adventures of Tom Sawyer**. Indeed, much of the book so closely resembles autobiography that it is difficult to tell where fact ends and fiction begins. Critics agree that Tom Sawyer was drawn from young Twain and two of his friends. Likewise, Aunt Polly was modeled after the author's mother; Becky Thatcher after an early sweetheart; Injun Joe after a local scalawag; and Huck Finn after the good-hearted son of the town drunkard. Published in 1876, **Tom Sawyer** was an immediate popular and critical success. Like Twain's earlier efforts, it broke with the genteel, romantic tradition that had dominated American literature in the mid-1800s. Twain had little use for the stuffy style and heavy-handed moralizing of his contemporary writers; instead, his works were based on real life. Readers at the time rejoiced in Twain's believable characters, realistic dialogue, and remarkable attention to detail. Although he was an early proponent of realism, Twain was also a master of humor and satire. As a result, his style — a blending further affected by a deep desire for social justice — is unique in its irreverence, exuberance, zest, and love of life. **Tom Sawyer** was followed by a number of successful and widely acclaimed works, among them *The Prince and the Pauper* (1882) and *The Adventures of Huckleberry Finn* (1884). Twain's later years, however, were marked by growing pessimism, and many of his subsequent books (including two **Tom Sawyer** sequels) are regarded as feeble echoes of his early work. Nevertheless, Twain is considered one of the world's greatest writers. His characters, perhaps the best-loved in literature, continue to delight readers both young and old, and his tales remain stories for all times. Twain's enduring appeal might best be summed up by his observation about **Tom Sawyer**: "Although (it) is intended mainly for boys and girls, I hope it will not be shunned by adults... for part of my plan has been to try to pleasantly remind adults of what they once were themselves, and of how they felt and acted and talked, and what queer enterprises they sometimes engaged in."

The Adventures of Tom Sawyer
Classics Illustrated, Number 9

Wade Roberts, Editorial Director
Alex Wald, Art Director
Michael McCormick, Production Manager

PRINTING HISTORY
1st edition published May 1990

For information, address: First Publishing, Inc., 435 North LaSalle St., Chicago, Illinois 60610.

ISBN 0-425-12241-7

Distributed by Berkley Sales & Marketing, a division of The Berkley Publishing Group, 200 Madison Avenue, New York, New York 10016.

Printed in the United States of America
1 2 3 4 5 6 7 8 9 0

BETTER LOOK OUT WHO YOU'RE FOOLIN' WITH NEXT TIME!

A fellow's got to be careful. A glorious victory can easily turn into defeat with...

...a dirt clod...

...and a fast retreat.

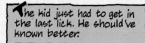

The kid just had to get in the last lick. He should've known better.

I'LL GET HIM BUT GOOD NEXT TIME. I'LL GET A POCKETFUL OF ROCKS 'N' FIND WHERE HE LIVES...

OH, LORDY! WHAT IF HE DON'T LIVE AROUND HERE? JUST VISITIN' OR SOMETHIN'... THEN I'LL TRACK HIM DOWN...

HE WON'T GET AWAY...

OOPS!

AUNT POLLY!

JUST LOOK AT THE STATE OF YOU! THAT'S IT! YOU'RE WORKIN' TOMORROW, YOUNG MAN. NOW GET IN BED!

Funny thing, but a body knows when it's a day off. The sun is brighter, you can hear more birds...

...or it just smells different from a school day. Tom had almost forgotten...

...Aunt Polly's resolution to turn today into a day of captivity and hard labor.

OH, NO... THIS'LL KILL ME. THEY'LL FIND ME LYIN' DEAD HALFWAY THROUGH.

Aunt Polly's punishment: whitewash the fence.

SAY, JIM? I'LL FETCH THE WATER IF YOU WHITEWASH SOME.

YOUR AUNT POLLY TOL' ME, JIM DON'T YOU GO TALKIN' TO THAT TOM--HE'S TO TEND TO THE WHITEWASHIN'!

OH, NEVER YOU MIND WHAT SHE SAID. 'SIDES SHE WOULDN'T EVEN KNOW. HEY, JIM...

8

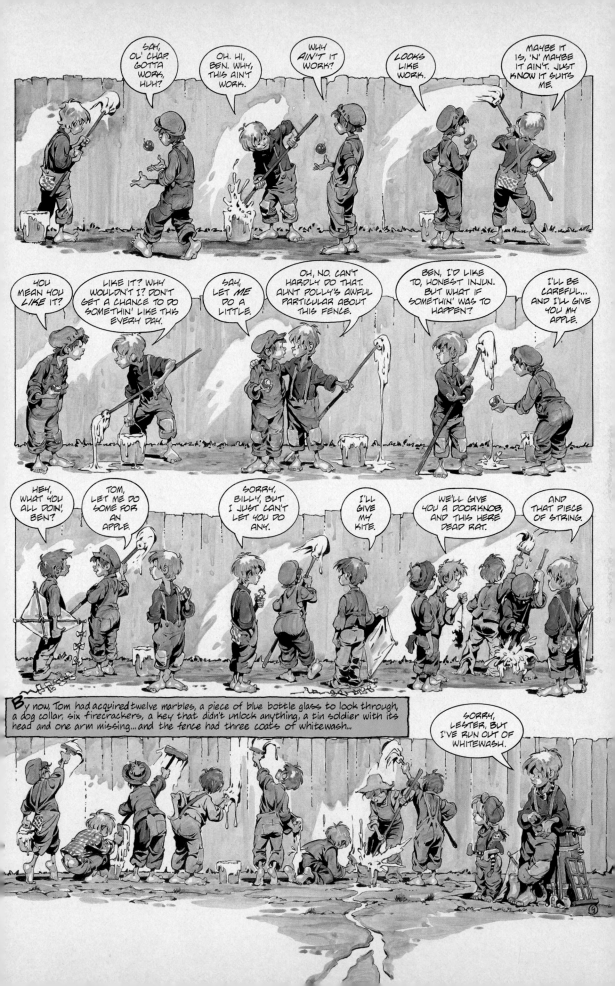

IT'S ALL DONE, AUNT POLLY. CAN I GO PLAY NOW?

DON'T YOU LIE TO ME, TOM SAWYER.

WHY... I AIN'T, AUNT POLLY. YOU JUST COME LOOK.

WELL, I NEVER! TOM, YOU CAN WORK WHEN YOU PUT A MIND TO, BUT IT'S POWERFUL SELDOM YOU'VE A MIND TO.

IT WEREN'T ALL THAT HARD. I'D SURE LIKE SOME DOUGHNUTS, AUNT POLLY.

I'LL WHIP UP A BATCH FOR SUPPER. BUT DON'T YOU BE LATE OR I'LL TAN YOUR HIDE.

NOW, HOW'D HE PAINT THAT WHOLE FENCE? I JUST KNOW THAT BOY IS UP TO NO GOOD. I CAN FEEL IT IN MY BONES.

STOP ACTIN' LIKE A BATH IS SOME FORM OF PUNISHMENT.

The Saturday night bath was just the beginning. Sunday morning meant squeezing into good clothes and shoes. And how Tom hated shoes...

MORNIN' MISS POLLY. YOU GOT SOME FINE-LOOKIN' BOYS THERE.

(10)

Being able to spit in a clever manner has always been a great asset to a boy's character. And Tom was no exception!

But this morning, his attention was drawn to the old pig shed.

If you hadn't known better, you'd have thought it was a bundle of old rags flying out of that loft...

But it wasn't. It was every mother's dread--Huckleberry Finn, Tom's best friend. Being homeless, he pretty much came and went as he pleased.

A real free spirit. Old Huck's lifestyle had made him the idol of every boy in town.

Although Tom was under strict orders not to play with Huck, he did so at every chance.

HELLO, HUCK. WHAT YOU GOT THERE?

HELLO, YOURSELF, 'N' SEE HOW YOU LIKE IT. GUESS WHAT I'VE GOT...

DEAD CAT! BOUGHT HIM OFF A BOY FOR SIX MARBLES 'N' THAT SNAKE SKULL WE FOUND.

SAY... WHAT'S DEAD CATS GOOD FOR?

FOR CURIN' WARTS! SEE, YOU TAKE THIS HERE CAT TO THE GRAVEYARD 'ROUND ABOUT MIDNIGHT, TO WHERE SOMEONE WICKED'S JUST BEEN BURIED. WHEN IT'S MIDNIGHT, A DEVIL WILL COME... WELL, AS HE'S TAKIN' THIS FELLA AWAY, YOU HEAVE YOUR CAT AT HIM AND SAY-- "DEVIL FOLLOW CORPSE, CAT FOLLOW DEVIL, WARTS FOLLOW CAT. I'M DONE WITH YE!"

SOUNDS RIGHT. YOU EVER TRY IT?

NO, BUT OL' MOTHER HOPKINS TOLD ME IT WAS SO.

I RECKON SHE'S RIGHT, 'CUZ SHE'S A WITCH! SHE WITCHED MY OL' DAD. HE CAME ALONG ONE DAY 'N' SEES SHE'S A-WITCHIN' HIM...SO HE TOOK UP A ROCK, 'N' IF'N SHE HADN'T DODGED, HE'D'VE GOT HER. WELL, THAT NIGHT, HE ROLLED OFF AN OL' SHED WHERE HE WAS LYIN' DRUNK 'N' BROKE HIS ARM.

THAT'S AWFUL, HUCKY... WHEN YA GONNA TRY THE CAT?

TONIGHT. I RECKON THEY'LL BE COMIN' AFTER OL' HOSS WILLIAMS TONIGHT.

BUT THEY BURIED HIM LAST SATURDAY.

THEIR CHARMS DON'T WORK TILL MIDNIGHT...THEN IT'S SUNDAY, 'N' DEVILS DON'T SLOSH AROUND MUCH ON SUNDAY.

DIDN'T THINK OF THAT. LEMME GO WITH YOU.

YOU CAN IF YOU AIN'T AFEARED?

AFEARED! 'T'AIN'T LIKELY. GIMME THE SIGNAL TONIGHT. I PROMISE I'LL MEOW BACK THIS TIME.

YOU BETTER! LAST TIME OL' MAN HAYS THREW AN OL' BOOT AT ME.

MIGHTY SMALL TICK YOU GOT THERE.

IT'S A PRETTY EARLY TICK, I RECKON-- FIRST I'VE SEEN THIS YEAR.

TRADE YOU MY TOOTH FOR HIM.

ALL RIGHT...IT'S A TRADE.

GOTTA GO, HUCK. SEE YOU TONIGHT.

12

THOMAS SAWYER! YOU'RE LATE AGAIN! WHERE HAVE YOU BEEN?

Tom's late arrival interrupted the introduction of the new girl in school...Becky Thatcher.

Uhhh... WELL, I... GOLLY!

COME ON! WHAT FEEBLE EXCUSE HAVE YOU CONTRIVED TODAY?

She was the prettiest girl Tom had ever seen. Amy, yesterday's true love, was forgotten.

I STOPPED TO TALK TO HUCKLEBERRY FINN.

HUCK FINN! THAT RAGAMUFFIN! YOU'VE BEEN TOLD TIME AND TIME AGAIN TO STAY AWAY FROM HIM!

THE CANE AND SIX SHOULD SUIT YOU FINE.

OK, THOMAS. NOW YOU GO SIT WITH THE GIRLS. LET THAT BE A LESSON!

Everyone knew the schoolmaster thought of Huck as a threat to the moral fiber of his students. So no one could understand Tom's confession. Now, I'm not saying Tom had it all figured out. But two seconds later, Tom squeezed onto the bench next to Becky Thatcher, the prettiest girl in town...

WANT A PEACH?

Uhhh... NO, THANK YOU.

13

Nudges, winks and whispers traveled the room, as Tom sat and seemed to be studying his book.

jake it
i got
more

IT'S NICE. MAKE A MAN.

NOW DRAW ME COMING ALONG.

IT'S EVER SO NICE... I WISH I COULD DRAW.

I'LL LEARN YOU!

WHEN?

14

Tom arranged to meet Becky during the noon dinner break.

They met up at the bottom of the lane.

OH, HI, BECKY.

HELLO, TOM. I DIDN'T THINK YOU'D COME.

DO YOU LIKE RATS?

NO, I HATE RATS. DID THAT WHIPPING HURT?

NAW...I'VE HAD WORSE. I HATE RATS, TOO.

WHAT I LIKE IS CHEWING GUM.

DO YOU? I GOT SOME. I'LL LET YOU CHEW IT FOR A WHILE IF YOU GIVE IT BACK.

SURE, I WILL. ALL YOU HAVE TO DO IS SAY SO.

SAY, BECKY... WAS YOU EVER ENGAGED?

NO. WHAT'S IT LIKE?

IT AIN'T LIKE ANYTHING. YOU JUST TELL A BOY YOU WON'T LIKE ANYBODY BUT HIM, EVER. THEN YOU KISS...

KISS?! WHAT FOR?

WELL, THEY ALWAYS DO-- EVERYBODY THAT LOVES EACH OTHER. DO YOU LOVE ME?

I SHAN'T TELL YOU.

SHALL I TELL YOU?

NO! WELL, YES...MAYBE. OH, SOME OTHER TIME.

I'LL WHISPER IT.

I... LOVE... YOU...

NOW YOU WHISPER TO ME.

15

HERE, BECKY. TAKE THIS. IT'S A BRASS KNOB, MY BESTEST POSSESSION. PLEASE...

NO! JUST GO AWAY! I HATE YOU!

Tom was sincere, but Becky had no way of knowing. Any boy in town would have traded his best dog for that knob.

Nothing could have hurt Tom's feelings more. And going back to school was out of the question. So he headed for his gang's fort, deep in the woods.

WHAT IF I DIED...? THEY'D ALL BE SORRY.

IF I COULD JUST DIE TEMPO-RARILY.

MAYBE I'LL JOIN UP WITH THE INDIANS 'N' HUNT BUFFALOES 'N' COME BACK AS A GREAT CHIEF WITH FEATHERS 'N' HIDEOUS WAR PAINT...

THEN JUST WALK RIGHT INTO SCHOOL. BOY, SHE'D BE SORRY THEN, I BET.

NAW, I'LL BE A PIRATE!

SAIL THE SEVEN SEAS FLYIN' THE SKULL 'N' CROSSBONES! A BLOODY CUTLASS BY MY SIDE!

'N' JUST WALK INTO TOWN WITH TWO HORSE PISTOLS. THEY'D ALL SHOUT, "IT'S TOM SAWYER!"

"THE BLACK AVENGER OF THE SPANISH MAIN!"

17

GIRLS... I JUST CAN'T FIGURE 'EM. ONE MINUTE THEY CAN MAKE YOU FEEL GOOD ALL OVER, 'N THE NEXT, LIKE YOU JUST ATE A PECK OF GREEN APPLES.

I RECKON GIRLS JUST AIN'T RIGHT TILL THEY GET A LITTLE OLDER, BUT... SHUCKS, THEN THEY GET LIKE... AUNT POLLY... TELLIN' YOU TO DO THIS... DO THAT...

MEOW. MEOOOOW!

HUCK! I FORGOT ABOUT HUCK!

MEOOOW, HUCK!

MEOOOOW YOURSELF, TOM!

HUCK, I JUST THOUGHT OF SOMETHIN'... I AIN'T GOT NO WARTS!

SHUCKS, TOM. I GOT PLENTY!

Their pace slowed down a tad once the graveyard came into sight.

HUCKY, DO YOU BELIEVE DEAD FOLKS LIKE FOR US TO BE HERE?

I WISH I KNOWED, TOM. IT'S AWFUL SOLEMN-LIKE, HERE.

18

But one of them was human. It was old Muff Potter. And the other was Injun Joe—both drunker than toads.

HERE LIES HOSS WILLIAMS R.I.P.

THERE IT IS. HELP ME GET THE LID OFF.

SHOULDN'T WE KNOCK FIRST, JOE? MAYBE HE AIN'T HOME. HEH, HEH, HEH.

SHUT UP YOU DRUNKEN FOOLS. AND BE CAREFUL. HE'S NO GOOD TO ME ALL BUSTED UP.

The other was Doc Robinson, and he stood so close that Tom could have reached out and touched him.

OL' HOSS HERE IS A BIG 'UN. FIGURE HE'S WORTH MORE MONEY.

THAT'S THE TALK, MUFF! I FIGURE HE'S WORTH ANOTHER FIVE.

YOU REQUIRED YOUR PAY IN ADVANCE, AND I'VE PAID YOU!

YEP, 'N' YOU DONE MORE'N THAT. FIVE YEARS AGO, YOU DROVE ME AWAY FROM YOUR FATHER'S KITCHEN WITH A WHIP, WHEN I ASKED FOR SOMETHIN' TO EAT. DID YOU THINK I FORGOT, DOC?

YOU FILTHY HALF-BREED. I SHOULD HAVE HAD YOU SHOT.

HEY, DOC. WHAT ARE YOU DOIN'?

HERE NOW. DON'T YOU HIT MY PARD!

YOU DRUNKEN HALF-WIT! I'LL HAVE YOU AND THAT INJUN DRIVEN OUT OF THE STATE.

Like a rattlesnake, Injun Joe waited for his chance to strike.

Just then, Doc hit old Muff with Hoss Williams' headboard... Injun Joe seized the opportunity...Tom gasped for breath. It was as if that knife had stuck him.

HERE LIES HOSS WILLIAMS R.I.P.

YOU OUGHT NOT TO HAVE DONE THAT, MUFF. YOU KILLED HIM. BUT DON'T WORRY-- I WON'T RAT ON YOU.

LORD, JOE! I'M ALL COVERED IN BLOOD... 'N' THAT'S MY KNIFE! OH, LORD! I DIDN'T MEAN TO DO IT... I AIN'T NEVER HURT A BODY AFORE--EVER!

The boys bolted out of there like a blue streak. It was as if the devil himself was after them.

21

Their feet hardly seemed to touch the ground. They were running scared.

By the time they reached old man Murch's cowshed they didn't have a breath of air between them.

HUCK, WHAT D'YOU RECKON WILL COME OF ALL THIS?

HANGIN', I RECKON.

WHO'LL TELL?... US?

NO! 'T'AIN'T LIKELY! IF ANYBODY TELLS, LET MUFF POTTER DO IT.

MAYBE MUFF DON'T KNOW INJUN JOE DONE IT.

LORDY! THEN WE ARE THE ONLY ONES THAT KNOW.

'N' IF THEY DON'T HANG INJUN JOE...?

HE'LL KILL US! SURE AS WE'RE A-LAYIN' HERE!

TOM... WE GOTTA KEEP MUM ABOUT THIS.

I HOLD MY HAND ON MY HEART AND SWEAR TO IT.

NO-- THIS ORTER BE WRITTEN... IN BLOOD...

BLOOD! WELL, A BIG THING LIKE THIS-- GUESS IT'S ONLY RIGHT.

So Tom found an old pine shingle, and set to writing up the agreement.

Each boy pricked his finger, squeezed out a drop of blood, and made his mark.

Tom showed Huck how to write HF -- and the oath was complete.

Huck Finn and Tom Sawyer swears they will keep mum about this and they wish they may drop down dead in their tracks if they ever tell and rot.

TS HF

The shingle was then buried in a dark corner of the shed.

Tom headed home, looking forward to a warm bed.

The next morning, Tom woke up late.

Something wasn't natural. Aunt Polly should have called for him at least twice by now.

His breakfast was laid out on the table, but there was no sign of Aunt Polly.

AUNT POLLY?

COME OUT HERE, TOM.

I'VE A NOTION TO SKIN YOU ALIVE... I JUST DON'T KNOW WHAT TO DO WITH YOU.

A WHIPPIN'-- MAYBE?

23

I DON'T HAVE THE STRENGTH TO WHIP YOU... YOU JUST BREAK MY OL' HEART, TOM.

OH, AUNT POLLY. (SOB) I'M SORRY. I WON'T DO IT (SOB) AGAIN. IT'S JUST HUCK HAD THIS CAT, 'N'...

HOW COULD YOU BREAK MY BEAUTIFUL SUGAR BOWL? (SNIFF)

SUGAR BOWL?! WHY I NEVER....

DON'T LIE, TOM. JUST GO TO SCHOOL.

Tom was devastated. Poor Aunt Polly's heart was broken, and he was being blamed for something he didn't do.

WHAT'S THE MATTER, TOM?

OH, HI, JOE. NOTHIN'. AW, JUST EVERYTHIN'.

I JUST GOT A WHIPPIN' FOR SOMETHIN' I KNOW THE CAT DID.

I'D RATHER BE WHIPPED TEN TIMES FOR SOMETHIN' I DID THAN ONCE FOR SOMETHIN' I DIDN'T.

YEAH. ME, TOO. I'M THINKIN' 'BOUT RUNNIN' AWAY.

ME, TOO.

WHAT WOULD YOU DO? HUH?

Hmmm... MAYBE BE A CRIMINAL. YOU KNOW, LIKE ROBIN HOOD. 'N' JUST STEAL FROM THE RICH FOLKS.

'N' GIVE IT TO THE POOR. HUH, TOM?

MAYBE.

TOM! TOM! WAIT UP!

THEY JUST ARRESTED MUFF POTTER FOR MURDER. YOU KNOW WHAT THAT MEANS.

THEY'LL HANG HIM... BUT WHAT CAN WE DO?

24

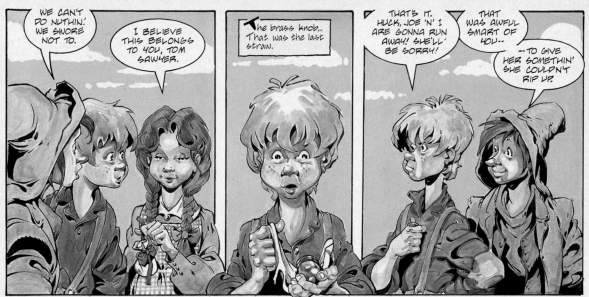

WE CAN'T DO NUTHIN.' WE SWORE NOT TO.

I BELIEVE THIS BELONGS TO YOU, TOM SAWYER.

The brass knob... That was the last straw.

THAT'S IT. HUCK, JOE 'N' I ARE GONNA RUN AWAY! SHE'LL BE SORRY!

THAT WAS AWFUL SMART OF YOU--

--TO GIVE HER SOMETHIN' SHE COULDN'T RIP UP.

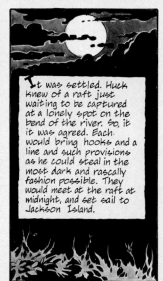

It was settled. Huck knew of a raft just waiting to be captured at a lonely spot on the bend of the river. So, it it was agreed. Each would bring hooks and a line and such provisions as he could steal in the most dark and rascally fashion possible. They would meet at the raft at midnight, and set sail to Jackson Island.

Tom arrived just after midnight. Crouched in the bushes, he hooted like an owl. It was answered by a bird whistle...then a voice.

WHO GOES THERE?

TOM SAWYER, THE BLACK AVENGER. NAME YOUR NAMES.

IT'S US, HUCK FINN, THE RED-HANDED.

'N' JOE HARPER, THE TERROR OF THE SEA.

'TIS WELL. GIVE THE COUNTER-SIGN.

BLOOD!

They raised their colors and shoved off--Huck and Joe at the oars, with Tom in command.

LUFF, 'N' BRING HER TO THE WIND.

AYE-AYE, SIR!

STEADY... STEADY-Y-Y!

STEADY IT IS, SIR!

LET HER GO OFF A POINT!

POINT IT IS, SIR!

25

The Black Avenger and his crew caught the main current, and sailed smoothly down stream.

LIVELY, NOW! SHEETS 'N' BRACES. *NOW,* ME HEARTIES!

AYE-AYE, SIR!

Occupied with their tomfoolery, they misjudged the current, and nearly missed the island altogether.

PORT! PORT! NOW MEN, WITH A WILL!

DARN IT. TOM, GIVE US A HAND?

They landed on a sand bar, a short ways from the island, and waded ashore.

It took several trips to get everything off the raft. The boys were exhausted.

But not too tired to make camp, take stock of their goods, and settle into a midnight feast.

WHAT WOULD THE BOYS SAY IF THEY COULD SEE US NOW?

PIRATIN' SUITS ME FINE. NEVER DID GET 'NUFF TO EAT, GENERALLY. IS THOSE PEACHES IN THAT JAR?

THIS IS GREAT.

THIS IS THE LIFE FOR ME. NO GETTIN' UP IN THE MORNIN', NO SCHOOL. DON'T HAVE TO WASH...

PIRATES, THEY DON'T HAVE TO DO NUTHIN'!

WHAT DO PIRATES *HAVE* TO DO?

PIRATES DO LOTS...
TAKE SHIPS 'N' BURN 'EM.
BURY MONEY IN AWFUL
PLACES WHERE GHOSTS 'N'
CREATURES WATCH IT.
'N' KILL PEOPLE...
MAKE 'EM WALK
THE PLANK.

WOMEN...THEY
DON'T KILL THE WOMEN...
THEY CAPTURES 'EM
'N' KEEPS 'EM...
ZZZZZZ

The next morning, all of nature was awakened to blood-curdling screams.

TOM!
THE RAFT'S
GONE...

THAT'S
ALL RIGHT,
TERROR
OF THE
SEA.

LET'S
EAT, BLACK
AVENGER.

Breakfast consisted of all of Tom's ham, corn pone, and most of Aunt Polly's preserves... except a jar of prunes, which nobody liked.

After that, they took a well-deserved rest in the warm sun. The only sound was the soft chirping of the birds until...

BOOM

CANNON
FIRE!

WE'RE
UNDER
SIEGE!

TOM? YOU WANT TO GO BACK WITH THIS CHICKEN-HEART?

WHY... ah... NO, HUCK, NOT ME.

I DIDN'T MEAN RIGHT NOW!

The mutiny was laid to rest, but Huck knew the signs. Homesickness was eating away at the two boys. Supper was eaten that night in dead silence.

Later that night, as the two boys slept, Tom was busy. He wrote two notes. One, he left for the boys saying he'd be back by breakfast. The other, he took with him.

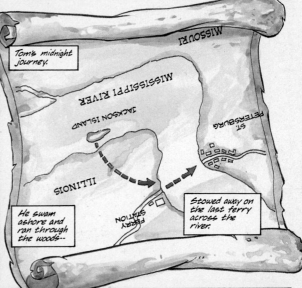

Tom's midnight journey.

MISSOURI

MISSISSIPPI RIVER

JACKSON ISLAND

ST. PETERSBURG

ILLINOIS

FERRY STATION

He swam ashore and ran through the woods--

Stowed away on the last ferry across the river.

An hour later, he was climbing over Aunt Polly's fence. There was a light in the kitchen--

So he headed for Aunt Polly's bedroom window. His intention was to leave the note and high-tail it back to the island.

But, suddenly, the door opened. Tom shot under the bed.

IT WASN'T A SPIRIT THAT MADE THE CANDLE BLOW. YOUR WINDOW'S OPEN.

29

OH, I MISS THAT BOY, MRS. HARPER. HE WASN'T BAD, JUST MISCHIEVOUS, LIKE A COLT. HE NEVER MEANT NO HARM. THE BEST-HEARTED BOY THERE EVER WAS.

SAME AS MY JOE. TO THINK I WHIPPED HIM FOR TAKIN' THAT CREAM, THAT I MYSELF POURED OUT BECAUSE IT WAS SOUR. THE THINGS WE'D DO DIFFERENT IF WE COULD...

WHY, I ACCUSED TOM OF BREAKIN' MY HEIRLOOM SUGAR BOWL. IT WAS JUST HE WAS ALWAYS LICKIN' HIS FINGER 'N' STICKIN' IT IN THE BOWL.

'N' I BET IF HE WAS HERE RIGHT NOW, YOU'D GIVE HIM ALL THE SUGAR HE COULD EAT. BUT...WE WILL LAY THE BOYS TO REST FRIDAY MORNIN'. BETTER GET SOME REST NOW.

Slowly, Aunt Polly got ready for bed. When she started to say her night prayers, it put Tom in tears. He wanted to leap out and hug her...but he didn't.

Finally, she fell asleep and Tom crept out. This whole adventure was a lot bigger than he thought it was.

Tom looked at the note. Suddenly, he had a better idea.

we are not drowned we just gone to be pirates
~Tom

He stuffed the note back into his pocket, bent over and kissed Aunt Polly. Then he made his stealthy exit.

Tom commandeered the ferry boat's skiff, and rowed downstream. He had a grandiose plan in in mind, and didn't notice the menacing storm clouds building up in the night sky...

The sky turned pitch black, then exploded with thunder and lightning. The howling wind turned the river into a raging sea. The rain poured down all night and all the next day.

On the morning of the boy's funeral, the skies cleared and the summer sun reappeared.

The hearse drove along the muddy street, with three empty coffins. The whole town was turned out.

Aunt Polly and Sid didn't sit in their usual seats. They went all the way up front.

When everyone was seated, the preacher silently raised his arms and everyone started to sing.

The hymm was always the same at funerals: "Abide with Me." Slowly, the door creaked open...

31

Three tired, wet and muddy boys walked down the aisle. The singing faded away to gasps of disbelief. Mrs. Chilvers, the leader of the Temperance League, let out a little squeak and fainted.

The preacher, thinking he was witnessing a miracle, turned a strange shade of blue.

TOM? IS THAT YOU?

IT'S US, AUNT POLLY.

The Harpers and Aunt Polly threw themselves onto the resurrected boys, and poured out thanksgiving. But Huck didn't know what to do, and started to slink away.

IT AIN'T FAIR! SOMEBODY'S GOT TO BE GLAD TO SEE HUCK...

AND SO THEY SHALL.

Tom had thought it was a grand idea to return for their own funeral. But he never figured it would turn out quite like this.

32

That adventure really took the wind out of Tom's sails. For a while, things really changed around Aunt Polly's house. Tom wasn't as averse to chores as he used to be.

Becky figured Tom was a real hero for bringing those boys back alive. She and Tom were seen holding hands at the "Boys Only" fishing hole.

BOYS ONLY!

The schoolmaster was positively amazed when Tom got a passing grade on examination day. At last summer vacation came.

There was only one thing that gnawed away at Tom.

HE ORTER HANG!

INJUN JOE'LL SEE TO THAT.

MURDER TRIAL MUFF PORTER

THAT'S RIGHT. I WAS THERE, 'N' I SAW OL' MUFF KNIFE THE DOC IN THE BACK.

DOES THE DEFENSE WISH TO QUESTION THE WITNESS?

NO, YOUR HONOR.

On the last day of the trial came a strange twist of events.

JUDGE, WE'D LIKE TO CHANGE OUR PLEA...

...FROM GUILTY WHILE UNDER THE INFLUENCE OF DRINK, TO NOT GUILTY. I CALL MY WITNESS FOR THE DEFENSE...

THOMAS SAWYER.

DON'T BE AFRAID, TOM.

I'M NOT, JUDGE, SIR.

WHERE WERE YOU ON THE TENTH OF MAY, AROUND MIDNIGHT?

IN THE GRAVEYARD, SIR.

WERE YOU NEAR HOSS WILLIAMS' GRAVE?

YES, SIR. HIDDEN BEHIND THE ELMS.

NOW, TOM, TELL US WHAT YOU SAW.

WELL, YOU SEE, WE'D GONE UP THERE WITH THIS CAT...A DEAD CAT IN A SACK...WELL, WE SEEN 'EM COMIN' UP THE HILL. AT FIRST, WE THOUGHT THEY WAS DEVILS...

IT'S INJUN JOE! HE'S THE MURDERER!

STOP HIM! MUFF PORTER'S INNOCENT!

34

I'M MIGHTY PROUD OF YOU, TOM. I'D'VE BEEN SCARED TO TELL 'EM.

I'M JUST SHAKIN' ALL OVER, HUCK. NEVER BEEN SO SCARED. HOPE THEY GET HIM.

The posse scoured the countryside for days, but there was no sign of Injun Joe. Tom knew Joe would be back for revenge.

WANTED—INJUN JOE DEAD OR ALIVE $2,000 REWARD

One night, Huck was bedded down in an old shed at the edge of town. He was awakened by low voices...

I FIGURED YOU'D BE OUT OF THESE PARTS BY NOW.

GOT A SCORE TO SETTLE. LET'S GET INSIDE.

YOU GONNA GET THAT KID WHO SQUEALED ON YOU?

NOPE. TONIGHT, YOU 'N' ME ARE GONNA BREAK INTO THE WIDOW'S HOUSE. YOU'RE GONNA BE A RICH MAN, WEASEL.

YOU CAN KEEP EVERYTHIN' YOU CAN STEAL. I DON'T CARE NOTHIN' FOR IT. I JUST WANT YOU TO HELP ME KILL THE OL' LADY.

KILL HER!? I DON'T GO MUCH FOR KILLIN' OL' LADIES.

THAT'S WHY I'M THROWIN' IN AN EXTRA HUNDRED—IN GOLD.

GOLD! WELL, I'LL BE! IT'S PART OF MURREL'S TREASURE!

I FOUND IT IN MY HIDEOUT. I WAS LOOKIN' UP AT THIS CROSS SCRATCHED INTO THE ROCK, 'N' FELL RIGHT INTO A CHEST PLUMB FULL OF GOLD. C'MON, LET'S HIGH-TAIL OUT OF HERE.

35

DON'T MEAN TO PRY, BUT DO WE *HAVE* TO KILL HER?

THIS IS *REVENGE!* THE WIDOW'S HUSBAND WHIPPED ME IN FRONT OF THE WHOLE TOWN 'N' THROWED ME IN JAIL. HE DIED 'FORE I COULD GET EVEN. SO SHE'S GOTTA PAY.

Huck waited until they were out of sight. Then he picked up his nimble heels and flew.

OH, LORDY. I GOTTA GET HELP.

he nearest farm was that of the Welshman and his two sons.

WHO'S BANGIN'? WHAT DO YOU WANT?

IT'S *ME!* HUCK FINN! QUICK, LET ME IN! YOU GOTTA HELP!

PLEASE DON'T TELL I TOLD YOU-- I'LL BE KILLED FOR SURE-- BUT SHE'S BEEN GOOD TO ME. 'N' IF YOU TELL IT WAS ME...

OUT WITH IT, LAD! NOBODY HERE WILL EVER TELL.

Huck managed to tell his story. Within minutes, the Welshman and his sons were armed and on their way.

It was just as Huck had said. The two outlaws were waiting for the lights to go out in the widow's house.

The silence was broken by gunfire. Huck didn't wait. He ran as fast as his legs could carry him.

36

It was dawn by the time the Welshman returned home.

WHAT HAPPENED? DID YOU GET 'EM?

GOT ONE--BUT THE OTHER GOT AWAY.

THE BIG FELLOW GAVE UP. THE LITTLE ONE MADE A RUN FOR IT. I THINK I SHOT HIM, BUT HE GOT AWAY.

HE GOT AWAY!!? OH, LORDY. I GOTTA TELL TOM.

WHY, HUCK-- TOM LEFT EARLY THIS MORNIN' WITH HIS SCHOOL FRIENDS FOR A PICNIC.

A PICNIC!?

The children had gathered earlier for a boat trip up the river and a picnic on MacDougal's Mountain.

WHO'S READY FOR THE CAVE?

COME ON, TOM. LET'S GO EXPLORING.

A bundle of candles was produced, and the boys pulled open the large oaken door.

Inside, it was as chilly as ice. The cavern's limestone walls glistened with cold moisture.

Some said the cave had no end, that it was a vast labyrinth of crooked aisles which ran into each other and out again-- and led nowhere.

LOOK OVER HERE, BECKY.

No man knew MacDougal's cave.

WHERE IS EVERYBODY?

C'MON. LET'S FIND 'EM.

By and by, the children straggled out of the cave. The clanging bell of the ferryboat signaled it was time to go home...

...no one noticed that Tom and Becky were missing.

Hours drifted on, as Tom and Becky wandered hopelessly through the tangle of passages.

HELLO!? IS ANYBODY THERE!?

I'M TIRED, TOM. CAN WE REST?

MAYBE WE SHOULD JUST WAIT HERE. YOUR FOLKS ARE GONNA COME LOOKIN' FOR YOU.

OH! TOM, MY MOTHER THINKS I'M STAYIN' AT MARY HARPER'S HOUSE TONIGHT.

I'M SO COLD AND HUNGRY. I CAN'T GO ANY FURTHER. WE'LL NEVER GET OUT OF THIS PLACE.

SURE WE WILL, BECKY. HONEST. YOU WAIT HERE 'N' HOLD ON TO THE END OF THIS KITE STRING SO I WON'T LOSE YOU.

HELP! WE'RE LOST! HELP!

IT'S ME! TOM SAWYER! IS ANYONE OUT THERE!?

OH-- NO!

38

Tom came face to face with Injun Joe... dead from the Welshman's bullet.

OH, LORD! INJUN JOE.

He was gratified to see him dead, but that made it no less horrific.

HOLY CATS! HE'S *DEAD!*

AIIIEEE

Although his candle had gone out, Tom realized he could see.

There was light. It came from the prettiest full moon Tom had ever seen.

BECKY! *BECKY!* I'VE FOUND IT! FOLLOW THE STRING!

It took all of Tom's strength to help Becky crawl through the small crack in the hillside.

The trial was over. Tom collapsed on the grass.

I'M A LITTLE HURT, BECKY.

OH, TOM. JUST LIE THERE.

BUT WE'RE SAFE NOW.

I KNOW. THANK YOU.

39

Tom passed out. When he woke up, he was safely tucked in his own bed.

Tom couldn't believe his eyes. Every important person in town was gathered around his bed. He was a real hero.

WELL WELL, YOUNG MAN.. HOW DO YOU FEEL?

I'M AWFUL HUNGRY, SIR.

OH, TOM! THANK YOU. YOU SAVED OUR BECKY'S LIFE.

HERE YOU ARE, TOM. READ ABOUT YOURSELF IN THE NEWSPAPER.

WE'VE SEALED THAT DARN CAVE UP. NO ONE WILL EVER GET LOST IN IT AGAIN.

TOM WILL BE ALL RIGHT, BUT HE'LL BE MIGHTY SORE FOR A WHILE. KEEP HIM IN BED 'N' GIVE HIM SOME OF THIS.

Huck was about to combust. He just had to tell Tom about his adventure.

CAN I HAVE SOME DOUGHNUTS, AUNT POLLY?

I SOMEHOW KNEW THAT'S WHAT YOU'D WANT. GOT A FRESH BATCH JUST READY TO BE SUGARED?

DON'T STAY TOO LONG, HUCK.

YES'M.

TOM, YOU GOTTA LISTEN. WHILE YOU WAS GONE, SOMETHIN' TERRIBLE HAPPENED! BUT YOU GOTTA SWEAR NOT TO TELL.

I SWEAR, HUCK. BUT I GOTTA TELL YOU ABOUT...

THIS IS IMPORTANT! SEE, I WAS SLEEPIN' THE NIGHT BEFORE LAST IN THAT COWSHED DOWN BY THE CREEK. WELL...

Then, without pausing to take a breath, Huck blurted out the whole story.

THE WELSHMAN THOUGHT HE SHOT INJUN JOE. BUT HE GOT AWAY.

HUCKY, INJUN JOE'S DEAD...IN THE CAVE. I WAS TRYIN' TO TELL YOU.

TOM! THE CAVE! THAT WAS HIS HIDEOUT! THAT'S WHERE THE TREASURE IS. MURREL'S GOLD! UNDER THE CROSS!

HONEST INJUN, HUCK? IS THIS FOR FUN OR FOR EARNEST?

THE MOST EARNEST EVER. THAT TREASURE'S DOWN THERE! HELP ME GET IT OUT?

YOU BET! RIGHT NOW, IF YOU SAY IT. BUT... HUCK. I DON'T... THINK I CAN WALK MORE'N A MILE.

LEAVE IT TO ME, TOM. I'LL FIGURE OUT A PLAN 'N' BE BACK AROUND MIDNIGHT.

OUT OF HERE, HUCK FINN! TOM NEEDS HIS REST.

The boys' favorite hour soon rolled around--midnight. And as he had promised, Huck had a plan.

Huck had borrowed an old mule from the Welshman. He strapped Tom to it. Huck loaded Tom and the mule onto the ferryman's raft, and rowed up river.

It was about that time that Aunt Polly went up to check on Tom.

OH, MY LORD! HE'S GONE AGAIN!

Meanwhile, up on the mountain, the boys hooked up a rig to the mule. This way, Huck figured to pull out the treasure.

THERE HE IS, HUCK. DEADER 'N' A MACKEREL.

LET'S GET OUT OF HERE!

WHAT!? 'N' LEAVE THE TREASURE...!?

YES! LEAVE IT! INJUN JOE'S GHOST IS HERE. HE JUST TOUCHED ME.

LOOK! THE CROSS! IT'S LUCK FOR US!

INJUN JOE'S GHOST AIN'T GONNA HANG AROUND WHERE THERE'S A CROSS--IS HE?

THAT'S SO! IT IS LUCK...

That's all it took to convince Huck. They crawled down under the damp rock...

And there it was. The Murrel gang's treasure.

I FIGURE WE SHOULD TELL FOLKS WE HAD TO DUEL INJUN JOE TO THE DEATH FOR THAT GOLD

HIM, 'N' AT LEAST TWELVE OTHERS.

42

MORNIN', BOYS. YOU TWO BEST COME ALONG WITH ME. JUDGE THATCHER 'N' THE WIDOW DOUGLAS WANT TO HAVE A WORD WITH HUCK.

HUCK AIN'T DONE NUTHIN' WRONG, SIR.

HERE'S YOUR BOYS, AUNT POLLY.

COME IN AND SIT DOWN. WE'VE SOMETHING IMPORTANT TO TELL HUCK.

HUCK, YOU SAVED MRS. DOUGLAS' LIFE. 'N' SHE FEELS OBLIGED TO TAKE YOU IN, GIVE YOU A HOME, AND HAVE YOU' EDUCATED.

YOU'LL BE ABLE TO GO TO SCHOOL. AND, AS MY SON, YOU'LL HAVE EVERYTHING YOU NEED.

HUCK DON'T NEED NUTHIN'. HE'S RICH! HONEST!

SEE! HALF'S HUCK'S!

'N' HALF'S TOM'S.

I'LL BE... IT IS A TREASURE! WHERE DID YOU BOYS FIND IT?

The boys recounted their story, and the money was counted. It came to a little over twelve thousand dollars. The townsfolk talked about it, gloated over it, and glorified it, all to a point of unhealthy excitement. Every deserted house within fifty miles was ransacked for hidden treasure. But none was found.

43

Mark Twain (Samuel Langhorne Clemens) was born prematurely in Florida, Missouri, on November 30, 1835, as Halley's Comet arced across the skies. His father, John Marshall Clemens, was a Virginian imbued with the frontier spirit and grandiose dreams of easy wealth. Intelligent and well-educated, Clemens' father spent his life in a restless search for profits from land speculation, barely supporting his family on his earnings as a lawyer and, later, as a judge. In 1839, the family settled in Hannibal, Missouri. Clemens' formal schooling ended with his father's death in 1847; he apprenticed to a printer, and began writing for a local newspaper run by his brother, Orion. Clemens worked briefly as a journeyman printer and writer in St. Louis, Philadelphia, and New York, before returning to Missouri in 1857 to become a Mississippi steamboat pilot (Clemens took his pen name from river slang for "two fathoms deep"). When the Civil War curtailed river traffic, he spent a short time soldiering with a group of Confederate volunteers. Clemens then traveled to Nevada with his brother, who had been appointed secretary to the governor. This trip west later provided the basis of his autobiographical *Roughing It* (1872). Moving on to California, he worked as a roving correspondent and collaborated with Bret Harte. His fame as a humorist and storyteller was established with the publication of *The Celebrated Jumping Frog of Calaveras County* (1867). Lecturing increased his reputation, but it was *The Innocents Abroad* (1869), the product of a tour of the Mediterranean and the Holy Land, that firmly installed Clemens in the world of letters. The success of this book also gave him the financial security to marry Olivia Langdon in 1870. They settled in Hampton, Connecticut, where Clemens began writing *The Gilded Age* (1873), *Tom Sawyer* (1876), *A Tramp Abroad* (1880), *The Prince and the Pauper* (1882), *Life on the Mississippi* (1883), *Huckleberry Finn* (1884), and *A Connecticut Yankee in King Arthur's Court* (1889). Bad publishing ventures and investment in an unperfected typesetting machine drove him into bankruptcy in 1894. To discharge his debts, Clemens embarked upon a lecturing tour around the world, during which one of his daughters died in Europe. Although Clemens paid off his debts by 1898, his writing began to exhibit a dismal cynicism. During this turbulent period, he wrote *The Tragedy of Pudd'nhead Wilson* (1894), *The Man That Corrupted Hadleyburg* (1900), and *The Mysterious Stranger* (1916). In his final years, Clemens became a bitter satirist. He died at Redding, Connecticut, in 1910, as Halley's comet again streaked the horizon.

Michael Ploog was born in Mankato, Minnesota, in 1940. He decided to become an artist at the end of a ten-year stint in the U.S. Marine Corps. He held a variety of art jobs before landing a position as a layout artist for the *Batman* and *Superman* animated TV series. In the late 1960s, Ploog became an assistant to renowned comic artist Will Eisner, working at Eisner's American Visuals studio in New York. With Eisner, he contributed for several years to *P.S.* magazine. In the early 1970s, Ploog ventured into comic book illustration; among his credits are *Werewolf by Night, Man-Thing, Kull the Conqueror,* and *The Monster of Frankenstein.* Since the late 1970s, Ploog has worked almost exclusively in the film industry, as a storyboard artist, designer, writer, and editor. Among his film credits are *Good Morning Vietnam, The Unbearable Lightness of Being, Little Shop of Horrors, Ghostbusters, Black Cauldron, Dark Crystal, The Thing, Superman II, Superman III,* and *Melvin and Howard. The Adventures of Tom Sawyer* marks Ploog's return to comic illustration.

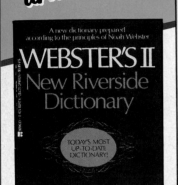
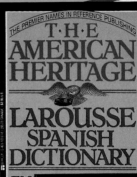